KU-074-539

Slobcat is our cat.
He does nothing but lie
about and sleep.

Heaven knows what
he does when we're
not there.

But when we get home he's still sleeping. That's why we call him Slobcat.

When it's his dinner time,
he's nowhere to be seen…

4 50
7 50
10 50
12 00
385
4 10
259 128
98
5 50
8 50

4 50
7 50
10 50
12 00
385
4 10
259 128
98
5 50
8 50

…and when we *do* find him,
he's even too lazy to eat.

I don't know *where* he goes
when we put him out…

…but he often comes back soaking wet because he's too lazy to shelter from the rain.

He spends so much
time inside…

…that he ends up getting in the way!

Last week Mum saw a mouse, so Dad put out a trap…

...because Slobcat
isn't interested
in chasing mice.

All *he's* interested in is lying about in the sun.

Luckily,
we don't have rats…

…because if we did,
Dad says we'd have to
get a proper cat.

Some people have dangerous animals in their gardens.

But for some reason,
they don't seem to
come into ours.

It's strange because
the *little* creatures
don't seem afraid.

Sometimes, when we're asleep, there are burglars about.

Thank goodness
we have Brutus to
frighten them
off…

…because Slobcat couldn't frighten a flea!

People say that all cats have a secret life that we don't know about…

…but I'm sure Slobcat's
much too lazy for that!